This

THIS WALKER BOOK BELONGS TO:

_____

_____

_____

_____

For Oliver

There are days when Bartholomew is naughty,
and other days when he is very very good.

First published 2001 by Walker Books Ltd, 87 Vauxhall Walk, London SE11 5HJ

This edition published 2002
Reprinted 2003

© 2001 Virginia Miller

This book has been typeset in Garamond

Printed in Hong Kong

British Library Cataloguing in Publication Data:
a catalogue record for this book is available from the British Library

ISBN 0-7636-8927-4

IN A MINUTE!

Virginia Miller

WALKER BOOKS
AND SUBSIDIARIES
LONDON • BOSTON • SYDNEY

George was carrying logs.
Bartholomew wanted to play.
"In a minute, Ba," said George.
"When I've finished,
then we'll play."

George was hanging out the washing. Bartholomew wanted to play. "In a minute, Ba," said George. "I'm busy now. In a minute, then we'll play."

George was sweeping.
Bartholomew got in the way.
He wanted to play.

"IN A

MINUTE!"

George said in a big voice.
"Wait until I've finished."

Bartholomew waited and waited.
He waited and he waited.

George was very busy.

Then at last, George had finished his work.
"I can play now, Ba," he said.

"What shall we play? On the swing...?
With your toys...? I know, hide and seek!"

"Nah, nah, nah," said Bartholomew.

Bartholomew fetched his little red cart
and took George to the woodpile.
He wanted to play …
carrying logs.

He wanted to play …
bringing in the washing.

He wanted to play ... sweeping the floor.

"Played enough now, Ba?" George asked.

"Nah!" said Bartholomew.

George fetched the picnic basket.
"Shall we have our picnic now," he asked,
"or in a minute?"

"Nah!" said Bartholomew.

So George and Bartholomew
had their picnic.

"What a busy day we've had," said George.
"You've been such a help, Ba.
Why don't we have a little rest now
and we'll … clear up … in a…"

VIRGINIA MILLER says of **In a Minute!**,
"In this book, it was lovely to illustrate Bartholomew's
independent spirit, and George's recognition that
even sharing the chores can be fun."

Virginia Miller is the author and illustrator of several
other George and Bartholomew stories, including
On Your Potty!; *Eat Your Dinner!*; *Get Into Bed!*; *Be Gentle*;
I Love You Just The Way You Are; and *Where is Little Black Kitten?*
Also published under the name of Virginia Austin,
she is the illustrator of *Kate's Giants* by Valiska Gregory
as well as *Sailor Bear*, *Small Bear Lost* and *Squeak-A-Lot*,
all written by Martin Waddell. Virginia lives in Wiltshire.

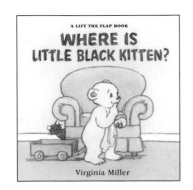